W9-BZX-479

Dear Parents:

Congratulations! Your child is taking the first steps on an exciting journey. The destination? Independent reading!

STEP INTO READING® will help your child get there. The program offers five steps to reading success. Each step includes fun stories and colorful art or photographs. In addition to original fiction and books with favorite characters, there are Step into Reading Non-Fiction Readers, Phonics Readers and Boxed Sets, Sticker Readers, and Comic Readers—a complete literacy program with something to interest every child.

Learning to Read, Step by Step!

Ready to Read   Preschool–Kindergarten
• big type and easy words • rhyme and rhythm • picture clues
For children who know the alphabet and are eager to begin reading.

Reading with Help   Preschool–Grade 1
• basic vocabulary • short sentences • simple stories
For children who recognize familiar words and sound out new words with help.

Reading on Your Own   Grades 1–3
• engaging characters • easy-to-follow plots • popular topics
For children who are ready to read on their own.

Reading Paragraphs   Grades 2–3
• challenging vocabulary • short paragraphs • exciting stories
For newly independent readers who read simple sentences with confidence.

Ready for Chapters   Grades 2–4
• chapters • longer paragraphs • full-color art
For children who want to take the plunge into chapter books but still like colorful pictures.

STEP INTO READING® is designed to give every child a successful reading experience. The grade levels are only guides; children will progress through the steps at their own speed, developing confidence in their reading. The F&P Text Level on the back cover serves as another tool to help you choose the right book for your child.

Remember, a lifetime love of reading starts with a single step!

For kids who have backpacks
—J.M.

Text copyright © 2015 by Julianne Moore
Cover art and interior illustrations copyright © 2015 by LeUyen Pham

All rights reserved. Published in the United States by Random House Children's Books,
a division of Random House LLC, a Penguin Random House Company, New York.

Step into Reading, Random House, and the Random House colophon
are registered trademarks of Random House LLC.

Visit us on the Web!
StepIntoReading.com
randomhousekids.com

Educators and librarians, for a variety of teaching tools, visit us at RHTeachersLibrarians.com

Library of Congress Cataloging-in-Publication Data
Moore, Julianne.
Freckleface Strawberry : backpacks! / Julianne Moore ; illustrated by LeUyen Pham.
pages cm. — (Step into reading. Step 2)
Summary: "Freckleface Strawberry and Windy Pants Patrick
make messes in their backpacks." —Provided by publisher.
ISBN 978-0-385-39195-5 (trade) — ISBN 978-0-375-97367-3 (lib. bdg.) —
ISBN 978-0-385-39194-8 (pbk.) — ISBN 978-0-385-39196-2 (ebook)
[1. Best friends—Fiction. 2. Friendship—Fiction. 3. Backpacks—Fiction. 4. Orderliness—Fiction.
5. Schools—Fiction.] I. Pham, LeUyen, illustrator. II. Title. III. Title: Backpacks!
PZ7.M78635Frd 2015
[E]—dc23
2014040654

Printed in the United States of America

10 9 8 7 6 5 4 3 2 1

This book has been officially leveled by using the F&P Text Level Gradient™ Leveling System.

FRECKLEFACE STR🍓WBERRY
Backpacks!

by Julianne Moore

illustrated by LeUyen Pham

Random House 🏠 New York

Chapter 1

Freckleface Strawberry
loves to go to school.
When she goes to school,
she brings her backpack.

Her backpack
has bugs on it.
Freckleface Strawberry
loves bugs.
In her backpack, she has

1. pencils

2. homework

3. gum

Windy Pants Patrick
loves to go to school.
When he goes to school,
he brings his backpack.

His backpack
has dogs on it.
Windy Pants Patrick
loves dogs.
In his backpack, he has

1. pencils

2. homework

3. a donut

Freckleface Strawberry's
mom and dad
did not know
Freckleface put gum
in her backpack.

Windy Pants Patrick's
moms did not know
Windy Pants put
a donut in his backpack.

They gave their children
a big kiss and said,
"Have a great day
at school, honey!"

Freckleface Strawberry
and Windy Pants Patrick
went to school.

Chapter 2

At school,
children sit
at their desks.

At school,
children open
their backpacks.

At school,
children hand in
their homework.

All the children had
the same homework.
They had colored in
their maps.

Almost all the children's
maps looked the same.
They were colored
and flat.

Freckleface Strawberry
looked at her homework.
Gum was on
her homework.

Windy Pants Patrick
looked at his homework.
A donut was on
his homework.

Freckleface Strawberry's
homework was colored
but not flat.
It had a big lump of
gum on it.

Windy Pants Patrick's
homework was colored
but not flat.
It had a big lump of
donut on it.
Uh-oh.

Chapter 3

"Time to hand in
your homework!"
the teacher said.

Freckleface Strawberry
and Windy Pants Patrick
did not know what to do.
So they handed in
their homework.

"Look," said the teacher. "Freckleface Strawberry and Windy Pants Patrick have something extra on their homework."

"Their maps are not flat,"
said the teacher.
"Their maps have mountains.
Good job.
You both worked
extra hard."

Freckleface Strawberry
and Windy Pants Patrick
knew they had not
worked extra hard.

They looked at each other.
"We have to tell her,"
they said.

Chapter 4

After school, Freckleface
and Windy Pants
talked to the teacher.

"We are sorry," they said.
"We did not mean
   to make mountains.
   We put gum and a donut
   in our backpacks.
   We made a mess."

"That is not a mess,"
the teacher said.
"That is only a mistake,
and sometimes we learn
lessons from mistakes.
Like how to make
mountains.
Or not to bring gum and
donuts to school."
And then she smiled.

Chapter 5

The next day,
Freckleface Strawberry
and Windy Pants Patrick
went to school.

In their backpacks,
they had

1. pencils

2. homework

Oh, and

3. bugs

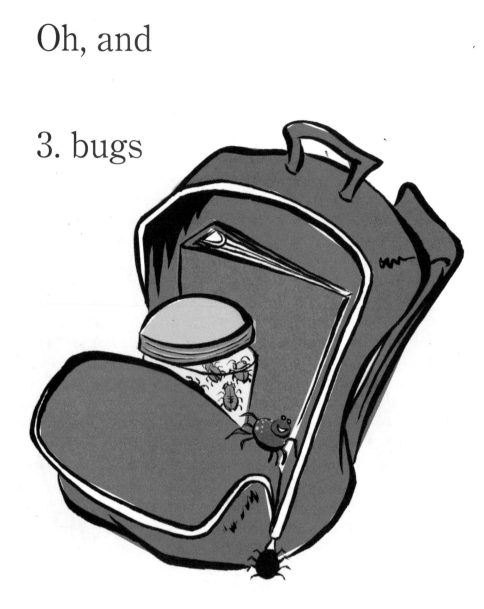

Freckleface Strawberry
loves bugs.